Note to parents, carers and teachers

Read it yourself is a series of modern stories, favourite characters, traditional tales and first reference books, written in a simple way for children who are learning to read. The books can be read independently or as part of a guided reading session.

Each book is carefully structured to include many high-frequency words vital for first reading. The sentences on each page are supported closely by pictures to help with understanding, and to offer lively details to talk about.

The books are graded into four levels that progressively introduce wider vocabulary and longer text as a reader's ability and confidence grows.

Ideas for use

• Although your child will now be progressing towards silent, independent reading, let her know that your help and encouragement is always available.

• Developing readers can be concentrating so hard on the words that they sometimes don't fully grasp the meaning of what they're reading. Answering the quiz questions at the end of the book will help with understanding.

For more information and advice on Read it yourself and book banding, visit www.ladybird.com/readityourself

Book Band 8

Level 4 is ideal for children who are ready to read longer stories with a wider vocabulary and are eager to start reading independently.

Special features:

Full exploration of subject

Richer, more varied vocabulary

Detailed illustrations capture the imagination

Longer sentences

Captions offer further explanation

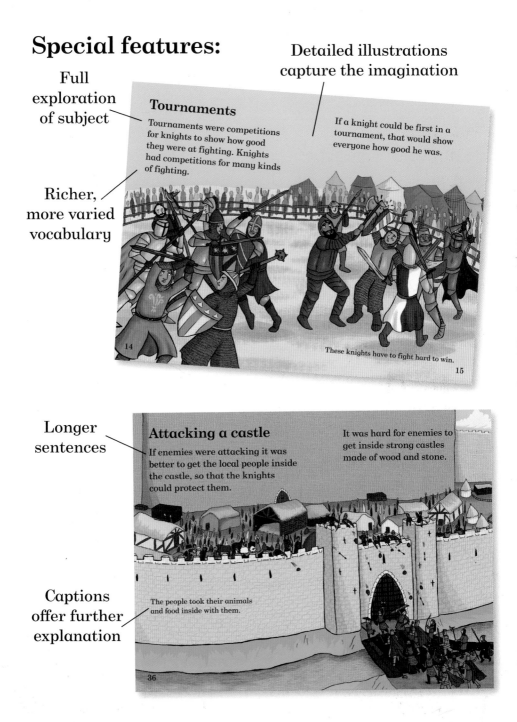

Tournaments

Tournaments were competitions for knights to show how good they were at fighting. Knights had competitions for many kinds of fighting.

If a knight could be first in a tournament, that would show everyone how good he was.

14

These knights have to fight hard to win.

15

Attacking a castle

If enemies were attacking it was better to get the local people inside the castle, so that the knights could protect them.

It was hard for enemies to get inside strong castles made of wood and stone.

The people took their animals and food inside with them.

36

Educational Consultant: Geraldine Taylor
Book Banding Consultant: Kate Ruttle

LADYBIRD BOOKS

UK | USA | Canada | Ireland | Australia
India | New Zealand | South Africa

Ladybird Books is part of the Penguin Random House group of companies
whose addresses can be found at global.penguinrandomhouse.com.

ladybird.com

Penguin
Random House
UK

First published 2015
001

Copyright © Ladybird Books Ltd, 2015

Ladybird, Read it yourself and the Ladybird logo are registered or
unregistered trademarks owned by Ladybird Books Ltd

The moral right of the author and illustrator has been asserted

Printed in China

A CIP catalogue record for this book is available from the British Library

ISBN: 978-0-723-29514-3

Knights
and Castles

Written by Chris Baker
Illustrated by Alexandria Turner

Contents

What were knights?

In the Middle Ages, 1,000 years ago, knights were soldiers who were good at riding horses and fighting in armour.

Knights had to have their own horses and armour, so they had to be rich.

The age of knights and castles was in the Middle Ages, about 1,000 years ago, from about 1000 AD to 1500 AD.

Becoming a page

It took many years to become a knight. First, a boy would become his father's page.

knight

page

As pages, boys helped their fathers all the time.

Pages had to learn horse riding and how to fight, too.

A page learning to ride a horse.

A page learning to fight.

Becoming a squire

Later, the boy went away from home to live with another knight and his family as his squire. Squires would learn about becoming a knight.

squire

Squires helped knights to get their armour on.

Squires even helped their knights
in fighting and tournaments.

13

Tournaments

Tournaments were competitions for knights to show how good they were at fighting. Knights had competitions for many kinds of fighting.

If a knight could be first in a tournament, that would show everyone how good he was.

These knights have to fight hard to win.

Jousting

Jousting was one kind of fighting competition. Knights had to fight on horses, and to try to knock each other down. It was very hard!

It was very hard to learn jousting.

Becoming a knight

One day, the squire would be made a knight. He had to be made a knight by another knight.

It was a great day when a
squire was made a knight!

Protecting the people

When the squire was made a knight, he could be the lord of his own castle.

He had to protect the local people if enemies came.

Some knights did not have their own castle.

These knights are not lords of a castle, so they are soldiers for another knight.

What was a castle?

For knights, a castle was a home to live in, but it was so strong that it could keep enemies out, too.

This castle from about 1000 AD was made from wood.

Later, knights had even stronger castles made from stone.

This stone castle, from later in the Middle Ages, is much stronger.

Who lived in a castle?

The lord of the castle and his family lived together with many other people in the castle.

Many people came to work in the castle.

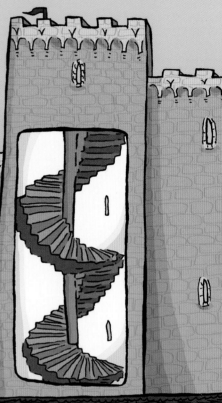

2

They had people to work in the castle, and soldiers to defend it.

25

Castle animals

Animals lived in the castle, too. Horses, dogs and falcons helped with hunting. Each castle animal had to work very hard.

dog

horse

Horses, dogs and falcons all lived in the castle.

falcon

Hunting

Knights and ladies hunted near the castle. They got meat for food and fur for clothes.

Knights and ladies hunted
animals with dogs and falcons.

Many ladies liked hunting with falcons.

Castle meals

Everyone had their meals together in the Great Hall. The food came from near the castle.

food from near the castle

People got the meat at this meal by hunting.

For special meals in the Great Hall, they could have things from far away, too.

special food from far away

Work in the castle

Knights had to work hard in the castle, learning to fight.

Knights and ladies liked their clothes to show that they were rich.

Ladies made clothes in the castle. They liked clothes made with fur.

When work was over

The people who lived in the castle did not work all the time!

These are some of the other things
people did when the work was over.

Attacking a castle

If enemies were attacking it was better to get the local people inside the castle, so that the knights could protect them.

The people took their animals and food inside the castle with them.

It was hard for enemies to get inside strong castles made of wood and stone.

Attacking a castle

The attackers could try to get over the walls, but that was very hard.

Sometimes the attackers would try to knock the walls down, but the walls were very strong.

The lord and his soldiers would try to keep the attackers out.

Protecting the castle

Sometimes the attackers would win in the end, and then they took over the castle.

Sometimes the lord could protect the castle, and the attackers went away.

This castle was too strong for the attackers!

41

The end of knights and castles

By about 1500 AD, other soldiers had got much better at fighting knights.

They could knock down castle walls with cannon. The knights could not defend castles against lots of cannon.

cannon

These attackers had lots of cannon! It was the end for this castle.

Picture glossary

 armour

 cannon

 castle

 falcon

 hunting

 jousting

 knight

 page

 squire

 tournament

Index

Knights and castles quiz

What have you learnt about knights and castles? Answer these questions and find out!

- When was the age of knights?

- What did a page do?

- Who could make a squire a knight?

- What were castles made from?

- Which animals lived in the castle?

- Where in the castle did everyone eat their meals?

Tick the books you've read!

Level 3

- Puss in Boots
- Angry Birds: Matilda Saves the Day
- Sharks
- Thumbelina
- Aladdin
- YOU won't like this present as much as I DO!
- The Elves and the Shoemaker
- Jack and the Beanstalk
- Furi on Music Island
- Poppet Stows Away
- Rapunzel
- The Red Knight
- The Jungle Book
- Roxy and the Great Escape
- Hansel and Gretel
- Harry and the Bucketful of Dinosaurs
- Angry Birds: Bomb's Best Birthday
- Angry Birds: Cheer Up, Chuck!

Level 4

- Dick Whittington
- Knights and Castles
- Peter and the Wolf
- Pinocchio
- I am Inventing an Invention
- Harry and the Dinosaurs United
- Heidi
- Katsuma and the Art Thief
- Luvli and the Glump-o-tron
- The Pied Piper of Hamelin
- Sam and the Robots
- Snow White and the Seven Dwarfs
- The Wizard of Oz
- The Little Mermaid
- Alice in Wonderland
- Oddie The Hero
- Angry Birds: Red and the Great Fling Off
- Angry Birds: Stella and the New Feather